Zayd and Maliha—
may your faith be greater than your fears.
—IM

In memory of Raheemah Yazdani.
—SKA

To my mother, Samia Abdel Mohsen, with love.
—HA

THE PROUDEST BLUE

A Story of Hijab and Family

Ibtihaj Muhammad

with **S. K. Ali** • Art by **Hatem Aly**

Little, Brown and Company

New York Boston

MAMA HOLDS OUT THE PINK. MAMA LOVES PINK.
But Asiya shakes her head.
I know why.

Behind the counter is the brightest blue.
The color of the ocean,
if you squint your eyes and
pretend there's no line
between the water
and the sky.

It's the first-day hijab.
Asiya knows it. I know it.

We're sisters.

The next day, I wait.
A new backpack, new light-up shoes.
I feel special. I feel like twirling.

Asiya comes out of the house.
And I stop.

It's the most beautiful first day of school ever.

I'm walking with a princess.

So I pretend I'm one too.

But even princesses have to stop to cross the street.

Asiya takes my hand in hers, says, "C'mon, Faizah!"

We speed-walk it.

Fourteen steps, fourteen light-ups to get across.

Asiya takes me to my line first,
hugs me goodbye.
I turn to watch her leave, give a little curtsy
to the princess going to the sixth-grade area.
She's easy to see.
Her hijab smiles at me the whole way.

My first-day hijab is going to be blue too.

"What's that on your sister's head?" the girl in front of me whispers.

"A scarf," I whisper back.

I don't know why a whisper came out.

I try again, louder now. "A scarf. Hijab."

"Oh," she whispers.

Asiya's hijab isn't a whisper.
Asiya's hijab is like the sky on a sunny day.
The sky isn't a whisper.
It's always there, special *and* regular.

The first day of wearing hijab is important, Mama had said. *It means being strong.*

I turn but I can't see the blue anymore.
I run to the big kids' side.
Twenty-seven steps to see Asiya.

I need to give her another hug.
I need to see her smile.

"Faizah?" Asiya's eyes wonder why I'm here.

"Are you excited?" I ask. "About the first day of hijab?"

She nods, smiling big, and I feel better.

Someone laughs from nearby.
A boy, pointing at Asiya.

Why?

Asiya's hijab isn't a laugh.

Asiya's hijab is like the ocean waving to the sky.

It's always there, strong and friendly.

Some people won't understand your hijab, Mama had said.
But if you understand who you are, one day they will too.

In class, I draw a picture.
Two princesses in hijab having a picnic
on an island
where the ocean meets the sky.

The girl who whispered in line says she likes it.
She says it so loud,
the teacher comes over to see it.

I wonder if Asiya drew a picture too.

Recess time is for five cartwheels in a row.
I land the last one
near the sixth graders.
Near Asiya and her friends.

Near a boy yelling, "I'm going to pull that tablecloth off your head!"

Asiya's hijab isn't a tablecloth.
Asiya's hijab is blue.

Only blue.

Asiya turns away. Her friends turn away.
They race to the middle of the schoolyard, their shoes
pounding the pavement, playing tag.

Mama: *Don't carry around the hurtful words that others say. Drop them. They are not yours to keep.*

They belong only to those who said them.

It takes me forty-eight steps to get away from the yelling boy.

After school, I look around.
I look for whispers, laughs, and shouts.

But I only see Asiya
waiting for me.
Like it's a regular day.

She's smiling.
Strong.

We cross the road hand in hand.

I can't wait to get home,
to show Mama the picture I drew.

To show Asiya that I'm wearing the same hijab in it.

Because Asiya's hijab is like the ocean and the sky,
no line between them,
saying hello with a loud wave.

Saying I'll always be here,
like sisters.
Like me and Asiya.

Ibtihaj's sisters, Asiya (left) and Faizah

AUTHORS' NOTES

Dear Reader,

When I was twelve, after I hit puberty, I started wearing hijab every day. Before then, my mother would have me wear hijab on special occasions and to school on the days when I didn't have gym. Having my friends, classmates, and teachers see me wearing hijab a few times a week made the transition to wearing it every day easier. Still, and even though my parents did a great job preparing me spiritually and physically for covering my hair, I faced bullying from classmates because of the way I showed my faith. I clearly remember one boy in middle school asking me why I was wearing "that tablecloth on my head."

It was at that time, in middle school, that I realized my faith had the power to change how people treated me and that I may be "othered"—all because of my hijab. You wouldn't think that a simple headscarf could cause such commotion, but throughout my childhood, adolescence, and adulthood, it has. It took me a long time to come to the place where I could brush off the looks and ignore the haters. It isn't easy, and I'm sure girls today face the same treatment—or worse—than what I faced.

I wanted to tell this story so that children who look like me could see themselves in a picture book—a story of family, love, and faith. So that they can see two sisters taking pride in hijab, and see that the parts of ourselves that might make us appear "different" are worth celebrating. So that children of color, Muslims, and those who are both (like me) know they aren't alone and that there are many out there who share our experience.

Finally, I wanted to say it loud and proud. My hijab is part of me—it's a testament to my faith and love of Allah. It's a tradition I share enthusiastically with my mother and sisters. My hijab is beautiful. To the young girls out there reading this story who are hijabis: So is yours.

Muhammad ♡

Working on *The Proudest Blue* with Ibtihaj Muhammad has been a dream come true for me. It is my hope that this book can serve as a testimony to the fire and love within ourselves, which all of us—not just those othered for observing hijab—can reach for in times of fear and sadness. As a Muslim, I believe that this love was put there by God to carry us through hardships of all kinds.

You are more than the whispers, the laughs, the hurtful words said. You are cherished and loved.

Put on your light-up shoes and land those cartwheels. And if you do it wearing your proudest color, all the more beautiful!

SK Ali ♡